The Quiddity

of Delusion

M.J. Nicholls

© 2017 by M.J. Nicholls
Book design © 2017 by Sagging Meniscus Press

All Rights Reserved.

Printed in the United States of America.
Set in Adobe Garamond with LaTeX.

ISBN: 978-1-944697-25-9 (paperback)
ISBN: 978-1-944697-26-6 (ebook)
Library of Congress Control Number: 2016955163

Sagging Meniscus Press
web: http://www.saggingmeniscus.com/
email: info@saggingmeniscus.com

THE
QUIDDITY
OF
DELUSION

HE PRECISE AND VERIFIABLE FACTS of this childhood incident failed to present themselves to me at the exact moment perfect recall would have benefited me socially. I was wilting around a table of wits and struggling to invent anecdotes that might have strengthened my standing as an "interesting" person—the first two improvised stories concerned public faux pas such as blowing a bag of custard powder in a supermarket and the hilarious-in-retrospect humiliation that ensued (complete with tittering girls and disapproving scowls from pensioners), and not realising my headphones had been disconnected in the national library so N.W.A.'s *Straight Outta Compton* broadcast to a roomful of embarrassed eggheads. These lies bordered on the unbelievable, and I read doubt in the smiling but unlaughing faces around me—authentic stories received wine-tickled titters and braying knee-slaps, and my success that evening hung on finding an appropriate moment to insert a real anecdote, otherwise I was doomed to dangle on the precipice of potential friendship and linger in my lies until the invites dried up and another door to social integration closed with a firm and committed slam. Usually, untrue anecdotes were constructed from fragments of truth and united into pleasing narrative form (as in arranging an autobiographical fiction) and the inherent deception in this act never caused me concern. I had blown a bag of Cup-a-Soup due to impatient ripping some time before, and the powder landed on my sweater and trousers (not my hair and face as in the anecdote), and would have caused embarrassment if another person had been around to witness the incident. By changing the Cup-a-Soup to custard I had added humour, evaded accusations of being a cheap luncher, and by setting the incident in a supermarket I had created a *bona fide* anecdote (imagine the looks I would have received had I told them about the time I blew a bag of Cup-a-Soup over my sweater and trousers while alone in the flat with no one to witness the hilarity, and the ensuing nuisance at having to dust off the powder and mop up the spilt specks with a damp dishcloth). There was truth in the N.W.A. mishap—I had been listening to music in a library (not the national one) and unplugged the headphones in error, although the volume was not so loud as to cause heads to turn and I was able to pause the track before embarrassment set in. The music was not hardcore rap but alternative rock (since the incident dates back to my late teens, the likely suspects are Radiohead, Sonic Youth, The Velvet Underground, or Joy Division—credible fare for a student). Whether or not these inventions were passable as presentations of the real me (I *was* capable of such mishaps), and whether or not the facts revealed (having to admit I shopped for powdered custard might have been riskier than admitting a fondness for rap) presented a truthful picture of me, this group demanded the natural veracity found in the anecdotes of the sort of loquacious outgoing people to whom a dozen amusing things happen per day. I had to lie. Telling the truth in social situations has never been and will never be an option for me because I lead the life of a writer and bookworm and cherish ritual and isolation like someone in training for a murder sentence. So my failure that evening to recall the precise circumstances of this childhood incident (that will function as the kernel of this story) meant I was forced into an heroic improvisation that no one around the table bought as genuine. I had blown my cover by exaggerating one detail too many, to the point one wit remarked: "That *can't* be true!" I wanted to explain how irrelevant the difference is between a well-told fictional anecdote and a mediocre-but-true anecdote, how the fictional anecdote holds more appeal since it answers to nothing but the imagination and, if presented within the bounds of the believable, pleases its hearers as much as it pleases the teller (who absorbs the pleasure from his hearers). I wanted to explain that the only reason the group preferred true anecdotes to fictional ones is because interesting things happened to them and part of their social dynamic was to outdo one another with wit and experience, and that their anecdotal style had evolved so that the small untruths each teller inserted into their tales to make them appear seamless were undetectable, and how the whole system was a social confidence trick and discredited the importance of fiction to enhance and replenish

The Quiddity of Delusion

everyday experience, which always fell short of the imagination wherein everything is permitted (if not socially). The facts are this. As a child I was taken with my mother, father, and sister to a small strip of beach in a coastal Scottish town called Burntisland (all one word so sometimes referred to as Burntis Land) in Fife, where someone kicked a football that displaced my ice-cream cone and hit me in the crotch. I was around nine years old. To pepper the anecdote, I lied about who kicked the ball (blaming a village meanie), that my swimming trunks slipped down as I clutched the afflicted area, and that five or six girls laughed outright at my pain including my sister (which was true—she laughed at all physical suffering I underwent as a child). Since I was willing to make light of this vulnerable and scarring moment in my life, the table guests laughed and offered sympathetic ohs, and the anecdote passed without damaging my chance to return to the group and establish myself as a regular, provided I cultivated an anecdotal style that fit into their accepted mode. When I returned home that evening I spent several hours analysing my performance, cursing my hesitant delivery, my failure to hit certain notes for maximum comedic effect. I began to wonder about the anecdote I had attempted to make authentic. What had happened that day, exactly? I had always known one fact of the incident to be 100% true—a ball of some sort collided with my crotch and I experienced some of the most excruciating pain I was to encounter until a basketball collided with my crotch in secondary school (an anecdote that can't be told due to the unfounded accusation

The Quiddity of Delusion

that the thrower—a ginger tomboy—was doing so out of spite, and the distinct possibility she remembers me, and the less plausible one that she might ever read this story and recognise a slanderous portrait of herself), and that my sister was in hysterics. How much detail hid in my memory? What effect had this football in the crotch had on my psychological development, and more importantly, if I was unable to recall the particulars of that pivotal afternoon(?), how could I be expected to construct a convincing autobiographical narrative about the occurrence, let alone convince the group with the telling of any memorable childhood anecdote? The group was unlikely to embrace me to their bosoms or any other desirable erogenous zones. I had made the mistake, in a fit of social desperation, when the façade of my antisocial loner's lifestyle collapsed without prior warning and I was up nights panicking about the decades passing without cementing lifelong friendships, of pouncing on the first social opportunity that came along on the internet—a series of dining events with strangers in affordable Bridgeloch restaurants—and spent weeks polishing stories to make me appear mercurial and able to switch between intense and incisive philosophical commentary, Wildean witticisms with relevance to the modern world, and humble-honest reflections on my life. Unfortunately, no opportunities to use these polished stories came up in the context of the conversations, and I had to fall back on improvised anecdotes and comment that showed up my ignorance and indifference to current events or anything outside my own literary efforts and explorations. The restaurant

The Quiddity of Delusion

was set up so that three groups of five had to sit squeezed into tables (the more expensive the restaurant the smaller the tables, legroom, and portions), and I was forced to sit beside four professionals who read no books—men who, if forced into choosing a book, would have found Dan Brown, Stieg Larrson, Ian Rankin, or George RRR Martin—men who equate popularity with artistic superiority, who might in all good faith believe Dan Brown to be at the top of his profession: a fact that inspired nothing but instantaneous loathing inside me before a word had been exchanged. The first sociable eater was Greg: the sort of ever-friendly everyman who has no problem straddling lowbrow or highbrow culture—content to sit in a panto shouting inane catchphrases or hum along to a Bartók violin sonata. The second eater was

Paul who was too vague to cause irritation and so deserves no more than a mention in this sentence. The third was Frank (the names have been changed to prevent libel—that is, assuming you believe the events in this narrative are true: I promise to have manufactured nothing in this set-up section that I don't admit to having manufactured—but that relies on your trust too, which is something I can't take for granted since this story thrives on sneakiness and a perpetual discourse as to what is fictional and real and whether that matters or anyone cares if it matters) and had a slight double chin disguised by a beard. His attempt to hide the oval nature of his face with facial hair only served to emphasise its comical eggishness, and I might have felt empathic towards him if he didn't wear his beard with such confidence—

never once scratching or tugging at the brown prickles in revealing tics of doubt but knocking back his beer and pasta as though the beard was unpresent and had been accepted by everyone as a stylish quirk of his appearance, never once checking for crumbs caught in the hairs or drying the dampness from the moisture on his beer glass, but wearing the damn thing with *insouciance*, as though it never even occurred to him that someone might accuse him of growing the beard to cover up his pudgy little face, as though he had never looked in the mirror and tugged at the flap of fat under his face and felt inadequate, as though he had the chutzpah to walk through life thinking no one would mind about his chin fat and people might even consider the beard to enhance an appearance that he might even in his vain lonesome have looked at and considered sexy and attractive—so I had no chance of respecting him. He was also an odd size and claimed to be a geologist, a fact I found peculiar as I couldn't imagine him straddling a cliff and inspecting rocks, not with that beard and stature. The final diner was Jeremy, who I hated the most. Jeremy was the shining wit (to my whining shit). Someone who worked in a newspaper office and had too many friends already, and saw no harm in butting in to my small attempt to engage with other human beings despite the obstacle I placed in my own way of disliking most people on principle for refusing to read experimental fiction and despise socialising. Jeremy thrived on social banter and the buzz at being thought hilarious (and knowing—believing with deep conviction—that he *was* hilarious) and made

The Quiddity of Delusion

pointless attempts to draw the less hilarious or inhibited social losers into his Jeremiac web by asking token questions as a means to prompt himself into the preplanned anecdote lingering on his tongue the minute the social loser completed his mumbling (to which Jeremy nodded along and ignored, using the downtime to mentally refine the timbre of the setup before the thigh-splitting side-tearing punchline desperate to zing from his lips). The selfishness of this social greed infuriated me. In a world where dynamic and attractive people (Jeremy was balding and no Clooney, fortunately) have first dibs on the friends and take far more than their fair share (and once these people have become "friends," their desperation to cling to the prestige of knowing a Jeremy closes them up to friendships with lesser mortals), there should be a law restricting unstoppable schmoozers like this from triumphing in an arena where novices flounder and are made to feel as though they should be grateful when a Jeremy deigns to speak at them about his merry-go-round life of endless antics that shape themselves into perfect anecdotes that need no rehearsing before the mirror and fizz off the tongue into the amused air and bring pleasure and admiration to all except the people like me who despise Jeremies and who will never say so for fear of making an enemy among someone who could crush his social future with a wittily timed epigram tossed into the ears of all nearby suggestibles. After that evening's failure, I wondered if I could ever make the beach anecdote authentic—that is to say, completely true to the best of my knowledge, and verified by those who were present

The Quiddity of Delusion

during the incident, and left to stand without having to alter the funniest details to make them properly funny, and told in such a way as to present a this-is-the-real-me portrait of myself, so that the hearers could embrace the-real-me and become closer to me as a friend since I allowed myself to be myself without the layers of fabrication and evasion (despite these layers being closer to the-real-me than the me that emerges when it pulls off a conventional anecdote told in a conventional way using conventional narrative). To achieve this, and understand the ramifications of that afternoon on the beach as to how I developed as a person, I would have to delve into my memory and dredge up as many facts as possible. The difficulty in doing this lies in memory's tendency to add untruths to the mix from other snatches of memory, similar incidents witnessed in life or in popular culture, and the fiction-writer's tendency to fabricate to the point he forgets what details are fabrications and what is the official version as verifiable by witnesses. I would need to consult my parents and sister, and return to the scene of the incident to see if being present stirred up anything. Perhaps doing so was futile—I couldn't reuse the anecdote with the diners, and even if I achieved a perfect story free from lies, no one would appreciate the effort I had put in to eliminating the fictional, and even if respect for my storytelling abilities doubled (which it wouldn't, of course, as people are too busy refining their own perfect stories and hoping to be accepted so that everyone ends up not accepting the others and waiting to be accepted themselves, and no one knows what

The Quiddity of Delusion

to "accept" someone in this situation means—I certainly don't, and have no real clue what I am talking about here either), there was still no guarantee of a social victory. What concerned me more was not being able to write narrative fiction direct from experience and engage the reader on an emotional level and not have to dump page after page of unfocused ramblings (as entertaining—or painful—as some of them are) on the reader in an attempt to contrive the authentic (as defined above). Or that all narrative fiction taken from the author's experience, or even straight autobiography, I had ever read was a lie, and that the only sensible way to poke near the authentic was to stop and question each detail as it appeared and to verify the facts with footnotes (containing witness accounts that could be corroborated or links to places where people could check each assertion by the author as to his past was true), or to create some kind of classification for works of autobiography, narrative non-fiction, or fiction drawn from experience that were not authenticated and so untrustworthy, or to simply drop the label of non-fiction entirely, and merge it with fiction and accept that recreating reality on the page is impossible and authentic experience does not transfer to non-fiction due to its subtle deceptions and lack of narrative oomph once infused with fictitious lies (whether subconscious insertions or direct insertions). Even the supposedly truthful parts of *this* narrative lack verification—since the Cup-a-Soup burst when no one was around to witness the incident there is no way this can be labelled autobiography, and since I sold my N.W.A. CD (a fact that can be proved by checking my eBay sales history, however, I have forgotten the log-in), the only evidence I once listened to this rap group rests on a hard drive sitting on my mantelpiece, where the music of over three hundred CDs resides in MP3 form, but even then—where is the evidence I ever listened to this CD? All that can be proven is that I owned and ripped this CD, and testing me on my familiarity with the lyrics is also useless, since I could have listened to the songs on the internet at another time (for which there is no evidence either). Even composing a fictional narrative leaves too much room for momentum-killing inquiries. And these can, of course, be expanded to encompass philosophical dimensions, such as how do your characters (who will have to be aware they are characters simulating "real" people), know they are who the narrator says they are, how do they know they are carbon-based lifeforms alive on the planet Earth, and even if this knowledge is made clear to them through verified scientific facts, why should they choose to be the characters the narrator says they are, or even if they are happy to pretend to be "real" people, why as "real" people should they conform to behavioural traits that are suppressing their freedom or making their lives complicated (for the sake of making the novel intriguing?). Upon sleeping that night (after the social failure), I began to have the sorts of nightmares that accompany fearful thoughts of not knowing the unknown. These nightmares, like most dreams, are incoherent remixes of the subconscious but contain interpretable scenes that echo one's waking fears and anxieties, or foretell future

The Quiddity of Delusion

incidents (if your behaviour like mine is repetitive and predictable), and can provide respite from or confound one's fears depending on the content. Not knowing the precise details of this beach incident became unbearable, since I attached to this not-knowing the paranoia that I would never be able to produce an authentic personal narrative so long as I lived and I always took comfort in the fact that I could at some point write an amusing comedic memoir and sell a few copies when I had grown tired of the relentless and fruitless experimenting I seemed unable to stop perpetrating in stories (having somewhere down the line made the assumption that it was better as a writer to be making new things and not poking commonplaces around the page and banking the lazy money for pleasing a populace of drivelling buffoons—if you are finding these insults tiresome, take umbrage from the fact that because you are reading this you are on the right side of the fictional fence, you are someone who reads long and self-contradicting tracts of mental effluent masquerading as a "playful" form, and derive some kind of satisfaction from doing so, which means you are probably somewhat unhinged and find the whole business of life utterly laughable and prefer art to living, which is the right thing to believe because it is what I believe)—not that it mattered to me that I could produce something that might sell, but some part of me believed that a credible writer is one who can sell their product, despite the obvious fact that shit sells and perfumed works of perfect art are buried under a mound of corpses, set alight, paved over, and turned into

The Quiddity of Delusion

shopping malls and car parks. I became fixated on uncovering the exact details of the Burntisland trip. I decided to visit the town first, before conducting the family interviews, to see if details returned to me. After procrastinating for several weeks (to get to Burntisland involves taking a train from Glasgow Queen Street to Edinburgh Haymarket and a train from there to Burntisland—a duration of one hour and forty-five minutes, and £20 for a return ticket), I made the trip. Setting off at nine o'clock, I boarded the train to Edinburgh with a sense of futile depression mounting. I was making this trip as an attempt to dam up a nagging uncertainty, and also thinking about the ways in which I could use the trip in a narrative nonfiction work that I might be able to sell to a mainstream publisher. I took notes on the train (since I was too distracted to read) about things I might include. 1) Sardonic descriptions of the town's bleakness from the point of view of an enlightened urbanite returning to a small place his intellect has grown too big for. 2) Sardonic character sketches of the sort of hilarious eccentrics that lived there. 3) Sardonic dismissals of the simple nature of life there, i.e. lack of cultural stimulation. 4) Sardonic descriptions of the sort of depression that rose up in me once I stepped back onto the beach into those surroundings again. 5) Sardonic digressions about the town's history. I was shooting for a sardonic tone. It also occurred to me that the trip could be sculpted into an anecdote I could reuse around the diners—a sort of sequel to the botched original where I describe in authentic detail the amusing happenings that happened

The Quiddity of Delusion

that afternoon (assuming amusing happenings would happen, which I assumed they wouldn't, so having to fabricate before the diners once again and make a trip back to Burntisland to recreate what didn't happen the afternoon of the attempt to remember the facts of the original failed anecdote and so on *ad infinitum*). I would have to confess to the diners that my motivation for taking a trip back to Burntisland was to render an anecdote that had failed to impress them authentic, and that I was making the trip to alleviate the fear that not knowing about this incident might determine my future as a fiction writer (and since all I really had in my life was books and my fiction—my entire future as a human being). The delusion behind this would be exposed. The delusion that I believed for a moment that those were the *real* reasons for making this trip—my real motive to attempt to write a literary work based on the experience. Once the seed had been planted that I could, theoretically, turn this incident into a literary work of some sort, my fiction-writer's mind began making structural maps and thinking up ways to incorporate all the stylistic tics I like to indulge in and detached itself entirely from any real emotional reasons I might have had for going back to this place (which may very well have manifested themselves when I arrived at Burntisland), and the trip lost all its personal magic to cynical exploitation. If you Google Burntisland, the first image is of the small strip of beach with the buildings looking pretty when offset by the hills in the distance, an image that contradicts my earlier description of the place being bleak. There are also pictures

The Quiddity of Delusion

of the famous (to locals) funfair that Burntisland (at the time of writing) hosts every year to attract the out-of-towners, where the central green is invaded by all manner of mustard-spired rides and oversize slides, along with the traditional funfair fare of candyfloss, shooting targets with bagged goldfish as the prize (that end up being poured back into the water when the kids realise carrying them around for the whole afternoon and in the car back home is far too burdensome for a so-called "prize"), and blaring pop music to soften (or muffle) the continuous sound of shrieking from people on the rides so newcomers aren't put off by the occasional panicky distressed wail, fearful scream, or extravagant retching sound. The beach incident took place during a funfair summer, so when I returned to the town during a quiet period in autumn it was difficult to immerse myself in a similar experience (since the next funfair would require a waiting period of ten months, there was no other option but to go during a quiet time), as the funfair sounds may have been an effective memory trigger. As I walked into the central green I saw only a few figures knocking about (I arrived about 2.15 on Tuesday afternoon so these were either retired people walking dogs or unemployed locals out on walks) and the cold wind made me regret not bringing a woolly hat. I returned to the beach and sat on one of the benches as visible in the Google images. The coastal wind made lingering unpleasant (since I was *sans* hat) and I was too embarrassed to climb down onto the beach while someone was walking their dog along the pavement there, so I dawdled up and down

The Quiddity of Delusion

the promenade hoping the dog-walker didn't stop to question me or make small talk—I have techniques to avoid this such as pretending to be deep in thought or looking at my phone or simply staring into the distance like an idiot who has never seen a distance before. Since the dog-walker was of an older generation, the phone manoeuvre might have met with disapproval in the form of a tut or sideways glower, so I simply feigned being deep in thought and offered the thinnest of smiles. Fortunately, the dog-walker passed me by, and I waited until he disappeared with his mutt under the tunnel entrance, and a few extra minutes to ensure he wasn't coming back for a second run, and went down onto the sand. Whether I was closer to the end of the promenade, or in the middle, is uncertain—I had vague memories of the tunnel being in the background, so that would place me on the right-hand side. The beach seemed far narrower than I had remembered—I had added extra beach over time, and since I was twice the height it had diminished naturally in proportions. The notion that anyone could fling a ball with such force on such a small beach against such strong winds seemed ludicrous— had I fabricated the whole incident? Since it took place at the same time in the day, the tide would have been at a similar position. I closed my eyes (and opened them surreptitiously to make sure no one had arrived and noticed me being weird on the beach) and attempted to reconstruct the whole scene.

There were people standing on the promenade people frolicking licking ice-creams talking trash making 1990s references the

The Quiddity of Delusion

sounds of background crowds the chatter and laughter and parents taming their children in Scottish accents and the distant sound of the funfair the shrieks and whoops and vomiting sounds and people spilling from the promenade to the beach

down   down
the   the
sidesteps   sidesteps

                 onto the not-so-soft sand

with kids   throwing   balls   digging up   sand
   making   sandcastles   toddlers   toddling about
parents warning them not to go too

                                                     far

     and me   and my sister with my parents
     me   sister sitting
     me   older by three years
     with an ice cream
     when
     I

M.J. Nicholls

see
someone   who?   where?
throwing
a
ball   coming   from   someone   somewhere
towards
me
and
it
hits
me   kids   kids   kids watching
in
the
crooooooooooooooooooootch
knocking   *a*
the ice-cream out out out my hand   *s*   *i*
                                        l
                                          i
                                   ng out my hand
                                        and my
                                        sister laughs

The Quiddity of Delusion

```
as I k
    e
    e
      l
        o
      v
    e
    r            HAHAHAHAHAAHAHAHA
      in agony   HAHAHAHAHAHAHAHAH
                 HAHAHAHAHAHAHAHAH
      (ow)       HAHAHAHAHAHAHAHAH
```

After this trip, I arranged a time to speak to my sister about the incident. I cited the story I was working on as the reason for our meeting (friendly catch-ups, especially ones lingering on moments from our tormented pasts, were rare). Since it was clear in my mind (smirk) that she had laughed at the ball hitting my crotch, it was possible tension might creep into the conversation if she chose to be unrepentant about that particular detail. This was even likely, since she is openly proud of her sense of Schadenfreude, especially when it happens to people she is close to, or if the person being hurt is vulnerable or elderly—this somehow increases the hilarity, to see needy limbs flailing on ice as the tears stream down their needy faces. To help me keep the concrete facts of the event clear, I made a list of the things that were indisputable about the incident, the things that were verifiable: one sister, one mother, one father, one me, one promenade, one set of sidesteps, one beach, other people on beach, an ice cream, an ice cream truck (somewhere), a ball, the sea, and a beach towel. My sister texted me on the morning of our arranged meet-up and told me she wanted to rendezvous at her flat instead of the mutu-

The Quiddity of Delusion

ally agreed coffee shop two minutes away from her flat. She had pulled this sort of trick on me before, and I knew some unpleasant scene was going to take place with one of her lovers when we should have been concentrating fully on reconstructing the unpleasant scene from my childhood. I arrived at her address at the end of Leith Walk (Edinburgh) and noticed an unshaven beanpole shouting abuse at someone on the third floor, his strong Leith brogue impenetrable under the volume of his explosive plosives, and I sneaked onto the leftside street to observe the aggro from a corner. I recognised the ferocious responses as issuing from my sister's lovely throat—in arguments her voice pricked up with hauteur and she viewed herself as the Rose to some junkie Jack, casting her latest paramour into the chilly death brine. To my annoyance, she buzzed him back into the building. I could either leave and pretend to have been held up by a train cancellation (I texted I was on the train twenty minutes before), explaining how I chose to cut my loses and return home after waiting four hours for a train (a text I would send from home), or I could enter the flat and deal with the latest errant boyfriend and hope to squeeze the recollection from her somewhere amid the histrionic mewling and prideless male pleading. I was impatient. I had already procrastinated and made a premature visit to Burntisland before I had the corroborated facts at hand. I buzzed and went up. The corridor was unclean but someone had bleached the walls that morning—mucky water pooled in the corners with dirt-tinged foam fading on its surface. My sister, Paula (not her real name), opened the

The Quiddity of Delusion

door. "Here he is! Maybe you can explain to him what you were doing with fourteen kilos of heroin in your briefcase and a rhesus monkey in our bedroom closet?" she asked. It began. Every visit was another drama. She was attracted to a certain kind of scumbag—helpless ones with enough menace to seem dangerous and sexy, who are always caught in some scheme that robs them of their cash and hope, leaving them attached to my sister like a blubbering infant—an occurrence that seems to bring her some degree of sadistic pleasure from the smirks that linger on her lips after bawling out another pathetic specimen of brainless manhood that she chose despite knowing full well she was choosing a pathetic specimen of manhood over a better one. This scumbag was named Dwerp (his real name—smirk) and had found himself involved in the lucrative trade of smuggling drugs in Paula's flat via inserting them up the rectum of a rhesus monkey. Apparently, rhesus monkeys had a layer of flesh in their rectum that made detection at customs impossible. "Come on! Give me a break! I was trying to make some money to pay you back, wasn't I?" Dwerp whined. "And do we believe that for a moment, brother mine?" she asked. I smiled and said it wasn't my business. Dwerp was eventually, after ten minutes of auricle-chafing disagreement, instructed to pick up some milk from the farthest shop he could find and we sat down to extract.

Me: "What do you remember about that day?"

Sis: "What day?"

Me: "When I got hit in the crotch on the beach at Burntisland."

The Quiddity of Delusion

Sis: "Oh yeah—hilarious!"

Me: "But I need to know the exact details for my story."

Sis: "Right, let's see. I remember it was the afternoon. Or early morning. Might have been early afternoon—"

Me: "Could you be as specific as possible?"

Sis: "What am I, the Memory Man? Or Woman? Trying my best here. [She wasn't—she was smoking and fiddling with her phone, sending several lowercase abbreviated swears to Dwerp on text.] I remember looking over and seeing the ball coming at you, and that look on your face of 'oh shit—I am about to get totally whacked in the balls with a football' and me collapsing in hysterics."

Me: "So you're sure it was a football?"

Sis: "Maybe. Could have been a beach ball."

Me: "But a beach ball couldn't have connected with the same force."

Sis: "Oh yeah. Hey, you hungry? Pass me a bag of Frazzles, will you?"

Me: "Fine. But focus. Was there an ice-cream van on the beach?"

Sis: "What? No. The ice-cream vans are near the rides. We got the ice-creams and ate them as we went to the beach."

Me: "Great! I wasn't sure about that. Do you remember who kicked the ball at me?"

Sis: "Yeah, it was that tinker friend of yours you brought along. D'you not remember?"

Me: "What? [This revelation made me forget her Frazzles.] I brought a friend along? There was someone else?"

Sis: "How can you not remember that? Daniel or Damon or something his name was. Do you really not remember the smelly tink?"

Me: "Obviously not. I can't believe there was someone I completely phased out."

Sis: "I don't blame you. He wasn't all that memorable. Your friends in those days were weird."

Me: "Do you think he aimed the ball at my crotch on purpose?"

Sis: "Dunno. Probably. He was a creep. I know he apologised after."

Me: "That's so odd. I suppose I had no idea who kicked the ball at me, but . . . how could I completely forget a fifth person?"

Sis: "You block out the schmucks. I'd like to

block out Dwerp, preferably with a very large block."

Me: "Ha."

Me: "What else can you tell me about this former friend?"

Sis: "Apart from that he smelled and ate worms and kept bats?"

Me: "No, you're making the mistake of conflating other former friends of mine. Mark ate the worms and kept the bats."

Sis: "What charming company you kept."

Me: "Yes, I take after you in that regard."

Sis: "I can't tell you anything else. It wouldn't surprise me if he flung the ball with the intention of hurting you."

Me: "He turned on me?"

The Quiddity of Delusion

Sis: "Yep."

Me: "Had I annoyed or offended him?"

Sis: "Look, he was a tinker from a broken home. Hurting people was what he did."

Me: "Fine. I'll have to think about it. Anything else?"

Sis: "I probably shouldn't have burst out laughing. It would've been funny if it was an accident, but I saw him deliberately throw the ball and still laughed. Not very sisterly of me. I should have chinned the little turd."

Me: "Apology accepted. Eighteen years late, but accepted."

Sis: "Oh—there's Dwerp back. You'd better go, unless you want to stay for round two."

Me: "Moseying."

This new piece of information changed the timbre of the entire incident. Instead of a humiliating beach mishap, it had become an act of traitorous violence between two supposed friends. The scene had taken on a dark undercurrent of envy and hatred. Why had this unclean oik from a broken home chosen to turn on me before my family, to sever a potential friendship with a clean and intelligent boy (although my personal hygiene and smartness weren't by any means exemplary)? The only motives were unthinking spite—if he'd been raised in a violent environment he'd have no qualms with casual pain inflicted for "a laugh"—or to right a slight I had committed against him. I had the habit with early friends to keep them at an emotional distance, being from a churchgoing background where manners and kindness were paramount, especially if they were torturing ants or worms, and I was supposed to frown on that sort of thing. It is possible I might have offended "Damon" with some display of hauteur in the car, or before leaving—failed to show my machismo or courage as a mischief-maker by refusing to utter swear words, breaking a glass bottle in a play park, or pass into some forbidden area. At any rate, I wasn't remorseful as to having hurt his feelings—a friend who hurls a hard ball at one's crotch is no friend at all (a popular proverb, first quoted in Montaigne). I decided, while I was in the mood to talk about the incident, to arrange a meeting with my parents to complete the official version of events before sculpting the nearest-possible-to-the-truth version of the anecdote as possible. I dropped in on my parents on my way back from Edinburgh.

My mother was pregnant at the time (at 50!) and my father wasn't sure if the baby was his (due a temporary separation that started three months before). I was hoping to postpone the drop-in until after the DNA test results were in but I had to take this opportunity before I lapsed back into inward brooding. When I arrived, my parents were in the middle of a living room skirmish—the remnants of sharded vases littered the chair behind which my father ducked as the windows rattled with their voluble disagreements. I stepped into the centre of the room.

MOTHER: "So pleased you arrived. Your father and I were discussing Chaucer and had a slight falling out over the Coghill translation."

FATHER: "Yes. We thought Coghill was shagging someone else and getting knocked up and suppressing the DNA results."

ME: "Did they come through?"

FATHER: "Oh no! Apparently, a herd of wildebeest stormed the GP's office before the results could be handed over and aliens abducted all doctors for the next seven millennia so we can't possibly ever find them."

ME: "Should I come back later?"

FATHER: "No, you stay there. Your mother will fix you up an egg sandwich and give it to someone else. Since she's so fond of leasing out her ovum."

ME: "Umm."

MOTHER: "Excuse your father. He's operating under the delusion that anything he says is remotely witty. What did you want to talk about?"

ME: "Well, I [explained the incident]. Any thoughts?"

MOTHER: "Hmm. That's a tough one. I remember you had a friend at the time, a chunky kid who smelled like an open sewer."

ME: "Yes, his malodorousness has been established."

FATHER: "Your sister burst out laughing."

ME: "Also been established."

MOTHER: "I remember he picked his nose. I hated your friends. Why did you always befriend the skanks?"

ME: "Because you chose to raise me in Skank Town."

FATHER: "Not chose, economic circumstances sealed our fate."

The Quiddity of Delusion

MOTHER: "Just shut up and make the sandwich."

FATHER: "I wish you had shut up and *not* made the sandwich."

MOTHER: "That's not even remotely euphemistic."

ME: "So what else?"

MOTHER: "I remember you being hurt, but neither of us were looking when the ball hit your balls. Your sister tried to persuade your father to thump the wee skank because she thought he threw it on purpose."

FATHER: "I came this close to thumping him."

MOTHER: "But you were too busy being a coward."

ME: "Who were his parents?"

MOTHER: "No idea. Skanks and dropouts. You can imagine the sort."

ME: "Yes. Did I know he'd thrown the ball at me?"

FATHER: "You believed it was an accident. Whether or not you believed it was an accident because you wanted to remain friends with the oik is another question."

MOTHER: "Another question would be where the hell's that sandwich?"

FATHER: "Why don't you ask your boyfriend?"

ME: "So I may have refused to believe he hurt me because I still wanted to be his friend?"

MOTHER: "You were desperate."

FATHER: "We always joked that you would end up befriending tramps."

The Quiddity of Delusion

MOTHER: "What are you telling him that for?"

ME: "Charming. Do you know anything about him. His surname?"

MOTHER: "Nah. I wasn't interested in learning his name."

FATHER: "Daniel, wasn't it?"

ME: "That was another friend."

FATHER: "Here's your egg sandwich, kiddo."

ME: "Thanks, dad, but I have to go."

MOTHER: "See, you weren't quick enough."

FATHER: "Thought the problem was I was *too* quick?"

ME: "Hope you two work it out. See you."

I considered the possibility of tracking down this beach bully, if merely for the sake of galvanising the anecdote when I came to the retelling. Tracking down a traitor and learning about his life circumstances might make for a more edifying story, and reflect on me as a more edifying person in general. If I turned up at his door, eighteen years after the fact, and he happened to be a slob in a string vest with curry stains, or a faceful of scars with fourteen brats crawling up his legs, this might not make for an hilarious tale, but a dark and pointless one, whereas if he had shunned his skank past and was a doctor or priest, there might be chucklier consequences. The task of tracking him down was immensely difficult, since I knew neither the first or second name. I decided, after these two meetings, and a few hours' contemplation, to cancel my RSVP to the Social Eaters, and let the matter rest. Now, you might find this

The Quiddity of Delusion

a damp denouement to such a searching and painful quest, but if you forced me to continue ferreting about in the fruitless sack of this narrative, I would find myself trapped in an ever-spiralling fiction, piling layer of fabrication upon fabrication until any kernel of possible truth became a long-forgotten daydream (*it was anyway!* I hear you scream), and this drooping dummkopfery became one fattening folio after another after another. I have chosen to sever the endeavour at the end of this sentence, in effect saving you the long slow descent into unimaginable torpor, and myself the very speedy descent into an obsessive voyage only remediable by a sudden cardiac arrest, or the sweet mercy of a brain-bound bullet.

M.J. Nicholls

M.J. Nicholls is the author of the novels *A Postmodern Belch* and *The House of Writers*, and co-editor at Verbivoracious Press. He lives in Glasgow.